#128339

128339 EN
Hansel and Gretel and the Cheddar Trail

Higgins, Nadia
ATOS

Hansel and Gretel and the Cheddar Trail

by Nadia Higgins   illustrated by Meredith Johnson

visit us at www.abdopublishing.com

Published by Magic Wagon, a division of the ABDO Group, 8000
West 78th Street, Edina, Minnesota 55439. Copyright © 2009 by
Abdo Consulting Group, Inc. International copyrights reserved
in all countries. All rights reserved. No part of this book may be
reproduced in any form without written permission from the
publisher.

Calico Chapter Books™ is a trademark and logo of Magic Wagon.

Printed in the United States.

Text by Nadia Higgins
Illustrations by Meredith Johnson
Edited by Patricia Stockland
Interior layout and design by Rebecca Daum
Cover design by Rebecca Daum

Library of Congress Cataloging-in-Publication Data
Higgins, Nadia.
  Hansel and Gretel and the cheddar trail / by Nadia Higgins ;
illustrated by Meredith Johnson.
      p. cm. — (Fiona & Frieda's fairy-tale adventures)
  ISBN 978-1-60270-574-6
  [1. Fairy tales—Fiction. 2. Characters in literature—Fiction.]
I. Johnson, Meredith, ill. II. Title.
  PZ7.H5349558Han 2009
  [Fic]—dc22

                                        2008038556

For Alice and Cecilia, another magical duo—N. H.

Fiona

Frieda

Chapter 1

Once upon a time in a land not so far away (in fact, across the street from the Forest Street Subway Station) there lived two third graders, Fiona and Frieda. The girls were best friends. They were also neighbors at Castle Apartments and in the same class at Sprinkledust Elementary School. In fact, Fiona and Frieda spent so much time together that many people thought they were sisters, or even twins (though obviously not the identical kind.)

The girls liked it when people asked them, "Are you sisters?" because it gave them the opportunity to pretend they were. And pretending was their favorite thing to do. They especially loved to pretend about fairy tales. For more than gum, more than picnics, more than water balloons, and even more than the last day of school, Fiona and Frieda loved fairy tales.

To anybody who knew them even a little, though, it was clear that they couldn't be sisters. Fiona and Frieda just got along way too well. It wasn't because they had similar personalities, either. In fact, the girls were quite opposite in one important way. Though they both loved fairy tales, Fiona admired the bright, sweet side of the famous stories: the balls and the gowns and the long-haired princesses. Frieda, on the other hand, was drawn to the dark side: the cauldrons, the spells, and the warty-nosed witches.

The girls were such a dynamite duo, a lot of kids at school were jealous of them. But Fiona and Frieda's classmates didn't even know the half of it. For, on top of everything else, the girls shared a special secret—their magic rhyming powers (MRP). They had discovered MRP while playing the Fairy-tale Adventures game they had invented.

That meant, for example, if Fiona said "sugar" and Frieda said "booger" at the exact same time, sparkles filled the air and the girls entered a magic realm of fairy tales. Their world looked the same, but all the ordinary noises went quiet. Only their voices and those of *real* fairy-tale characters could be heard.

Soon Fiona and Frieda were in the middle of a fairy-tale emergency, and they were the only ones who knew how to save the princess or get rid of the evil witch. Sometimes Fiona and Frieda got so scared they were tempted to use their magic powers to leave the fairy tale. In the end, though, they never gave up on the characters who were more real to them than anybody else.

Fiona and Frieda always had fairy tales on their minds. Today, at least, fairy tales were in the backs of their minds. This afternoon, the girls got to leave school early.

Both Fiona and Frieda were members of Girls United Troop 895. Their project for the day was to help clean up the city. The campaign was called Sparkle, Sprinkledust! (Fiona herself had thought of that title.) Frieda, Fiona, and their friends were going to pick up litter at the Forest Street Subway Station.

Fiona and Frieda squeezed hands as they stepped onto the long escalator that led deep into the subway tunnel. They felt as excited as puppies. Almost nothing made Fiona feel more like Cinderella than cleaning.

"Frieda, I think today is a perfect day for me to be Cinderella," Fiona giggled.

Frieda laughed. "Since we'll be underground, I wonder which witch would be best for me. Maybe I should be a troll! Oh . . . that's it!"

Fiona's thoughts had already returned to cleaning. Who knew what treasures were to be found on the subway floors? The subway had already provided many unique items for Fiona's treasure box—a deep red bead that must have broken off a necklace, a marbled pen cap, and a piece of sparkly blue shoelace, to name a few. Fiona had worn pants with extra pockets, just in case.

For her part, nothing sent Frieda's imagination into overdrive like the cool darkness of the subway. The rubbery smell, the echoing melodies performed by street musicians, the faces looming from the giant advertisements. . . . Here, Frieda could imagine the creepiest things.

At the bottom of the escalator, each girl was handed a pair of rubber gloves and a bright yellow bag. Fiona and Frieda got to work right away. They were happy to do their part on behalf of their fellow Sprinkledust citizens.

"Let's see how fast we can do this!" Frieda exclaimed.

"What about all of the cool stuff we'll find?" Fiona wondered aloud. "Let me know what you pick up, okay? I don't want to miss anything that might be marvelous!"

Fiona adored the word *marvelous*. It sounded lovely and important and full of potential. She decided that cleaning up the city was, indeed, going to be marvelous.

Little did they know, however, that their afternoon's assignment was soon to change. Their new task would prove far more important than even Sparkle, Sprinkledust!

Chapter 2

Fiona had a gift for finding the most wondrous items beneath the junkiest junk of Sprinkledust's streets. Already, one of her pockets had started to bulge. In addition to 43¢, she had collected two working pens (with caps), a stuffed-animal snake (with googly eyes), and the metal lid to a can of tomatoes.

The lid wasn't wonderful enough for Fiona's treasure collection, of course. However, with a little paint, it would be a great addition to the mobile she'd been working on. The only problem was that its edges were kind of sharp.

She coiled the snake around the jagged lid so it wouldn't rip the pocket of her pants.

In spite of her treasure hunt, Fiona was still able to pick up litter and chat with Frieda. "Eeeeeeeewwwwww," Fiona said to her friend as she squatted over a small, orange object. "Frieda, check this out!"

Frieda instantly recognized the shape of the ant-covered cracker. "It's a Cheddar Chimp! Mmmmmmm." She breathed in the salty, cheddar smell of one of her favorite snacks—tiny orange crackers shaped like chimpanzees.

"Look!" Fiona said. "There's another one!"

"And another over here!" Frieda said. "There must be a thousand ants on it!"

Frieda got on her hands and knees to examine the ant-covered Chimp. She watched one ant

disappear into a crack with a giant orange chunk on its back. Then she squinted at all of the ants at once, and the whole cracker seemed to ripple.

"Gross!" Fiona said. A trail of ant-covered crackers led all the way to the end of the tunnel.

One by one, Fiona started to pick up the crackers with her gloved fingertips. Soon she was halfway down the tunnel. "Frieda! Come on!"

"Okay, okay." Frieda tore herself away from the ant spectacle and caught up with her friend. She began to help Fiona scoop up the crackers and put them in the yellow bag.

Fiona and Frieda concentrated hard on their task. The trail of Cheddar Chimps led them around the corner, down another tunnel, down a flight of stairs, to the left, and then another left. Or was it a right?

As the girls worked, the trail of crackers got thinner until Frieda scooped up what appeared to be the very last Cheddar Chimp. "That's the end of the trail," she announced.

By now the girls' rubber gloves had turned bright orange. With a satisfied "hmmmmph," Fiona stood up, snapped off her gloves, and threw them in her bag. She looked at her watch. "I guess we'd better turn back now."

But Frieda wasn't listening. She was just standing there, as still as a house, her rubber gloves limp in one hand.

"Frieda?" Fiona said.

Tac. Tac. The gloves made small smacking sounds as they fell out of Frieda's hand, but she didn't even notice.

"Frieda?"

Fiona was starting to get worried now. She lifted her head and looked around. Now it was her turn to stand in shocked surprise, chills running over her body like scared spiders.

Gone were the melodies of street musicians, the whoosh of trains, the patter of walking feet, and the chatter of voices. Gone were the streams of busy people. Gone were the cheerful advertisements and the green signs with arrows.

Fiona and Frieda stood alone with nothing but their long shadows in an empty, silent tunnel.

To the right, to the left, ahead of the girls, and behind them, other empty, silent tunnels stretched into darkness.

"Which way? Which way?" Fiona asked, panic rising in her voice.

Frieda ran over and hugged her friend. "Shhhhhh," she whispered. "I hear something."

Over the pounding of their own hearts, the girls listened to a familiar sound—the even breathing of someone sleeping.

"Maybe whoever it is can help us," Fiona said. She was moving from panic mode to planning mode. "C'mon! The noise is coming from over there."

Fiona pointed to the tunnel ahead of them. Holding hands, the girls walked slowly toward the sound.

"Look, Fiona!" Frieda pointed at two figures slumped against a wall. The girls crept closer.

Fiona gasped. "They're kids!"

The sleeping kids, one girl and one boy, looked no older than Fiona and Frieda. The girl was curled up with her head on a stuffed backpack. The boy leaned against the tunnel wall, his backpack under his outstretched legs.

"They must be brother and sister," Frieda whispered.

Both the boy and the girl had the same straight, whitish-blonde hair. His stuck out in little spikes all over his head, while hers was pulled back in a perfect, spunky ponytail. They had whitish eyelashes, too, that quivered as they dreamed.

"They look like they're from a clothes catalog or a magazine . . . ," Fiona whispered back.

The boy wore green high-top sneakers, black jeans, and a red, satiny jacket with an American flag on the arm. The girl had her own funky style, with silver clogs, blue jeans, and a red cowboy bandana tied around her neck.

Fiona giggled a little as she pointed to the girl's glasses. The glasses were orange squares the size of postage stamps. "Those are cute, but how can she even see out of them?" Fiona asked, thinking of her own stylish pink frames.

But just as before, Frieda wasn't listening. She was too busy staring at the name tags on the kids' backpacks.

Finally, Frieda spoke, "Fiona, look. Look at their backpacks. You are not . . . going . . . to believe this."

Chapter 3

At first, Fiona just laughed when she read the name tags. "Hansel and Gretel! Just like the fairy tale!" she exclaimed.

But even as she said it, she realized her mistake. It wasn't *like* the fairy tale, it *was* the fairy tale.

"The trail of Cheddar Chimps," Fiona said slowly, "were the breadcrumbs!"

She ran through the fairy tale in her mind. In that story, Hansel leaves a trail of breadcrumbs as he and his sister walk deep into the forest. He hopes to follow the trail home, but instead, birds eat the crumbs and—

"We're doomed!" Fiona wailed.

Well, maybe *doomed* was too strong a word, but they certainly were in trouble. The girls had cleaned up the trail of Cheddar Chimps. So, just as in the story, they were lost with nothing to lead them back.

"And it's all our fault—especially mine!" Fiona wailed.

Frieda didn't know what to say. Usually she was the one to freak out during fairy-tale emergencies, and Fiona was the one who comforted her. For some reason, however, Frieda felt oddly calm. The quiet and the darkness helped her think.

"How are we going to tell Hansel and Gretel we ruined their trail?" Fiona gripped the sides of her head as if she were blocking out a terrible noise.

"A plan!" Frieda jumped up. That's how Fiona always got Frieda back on track. They needed to work on a plan right away.

"Yes, yes," Fiona said. That word *plan* had already made her focus.

"First we activate MRP," Frieda said.

"Good idea." Fiona twirled a finger in her hair. "Let's see . . . Number Seven."

She was referring to a list of numbered rhymes the girls had memorized for just such an emergency.

"Three, two, one . . . Hula hoop!" Fiona shouted.

At the exact same time, Frieda chimed in with, "Bowl-a'-soup!"

Magic sparkles filled the air and everything went even quieter. "It worked!" Fiona said, smiling. Frieda smiled, too. Her friend was back on track.

Fiona and Frieda meant to work further on a plan, but they didn't get the chance. The magic sparkles must have awakened Hansel because just then the girls heard his sleepy voice say, "Look, Gretel—fireflies!"

Gretel sat up and rubbed her eyes, but the magic sparkles had already fizzled away.

"Oh, it must have just been a dream," Hansel said, his voice a little disappointed.

But in place of magic sparkles, Gretel saw an even more welcome sight. "Hello!" She held out her hand as she ran to Fiona and Frieda. "Hello! Hello!" She shook hands like a grown-up. "My name is Gretel, and this is my brother Hansel." She pointed to her brother, who peered at them from his spot on the floor.

"Hansel!" Gretel whisper-yelled at her brother. "Come say hi!" As he slowly walked over, she turned to Fiona and Frieda and said in another loud whisper, "He's shy."

Hansel must have stepped on Gretel's heel for saying that. For the next moment he was beside her grinning, and she was hopping on one foot.

Hansel peered at Fiona and Frieda until they started to squirm. "Who are you?" he demanded.

"Um, Frieda?" The way Hansel looked at Frieda made her want to say everything like a question.

"And I'm Fiona." Fiona stared him down with a winning smile until he was forced to give a little smile back.

"Oh, Fiona, Frieda. Are you from Sprinkledust?" Gretel had stopped hopping now.

"Yes, we are," Fiona said. "But we don't know, and we're so sorry—"

"Wonderful!" Gretel interrupted. "Then you may be able to assist us. You see, we're vacationing in Sprinkledust, and it seems we've become separated from our parents. Your subway system is so very unusual, and I'm afraid we are quite flummoxed by its labyrinthine tunnels."

Fiona's and Frieda's expressions must have said, "huh?" because Hansel answered their unspoken question. "La-buh-RIN-thun means 'like a maze.' My sister sometimes forgets not everyone's a walking dictionary."

He grinned at Gretel and she glared at him. Then she pinched his side, which made him do a little dance.

"What Gretel means," he continued, "is we're over a waterfall without a barrel. We're trapped in a gorilla cage without bananas. We're on the top of a hot metal slide wearing shorts. We're, we're . . ." Hansel waved his arms over his head, as if to pluck the perfect word from an imaginary tree.

"Lost?" Frieda offered.

"YES! LOST!" Hansel shouted. "So lost we spent the night in this subway tunnel!"

"I don't understand," Fiona said. "Why didn't you just follow the trail of Cheddar Chimps back to the terminal?"

Now it was Hansel's turn to look confused. "What chimps? I didn't make a trail of Cheddar Chimps. But, I've been saving a bag of them right here." He unzipped one of his shiny red pockets.

"Oh, man!" Hansel turned the pocket inside out to show his finger poking through a hole. "All my Cheddar Chimps fell out!"

So Hansel *hadn't* made the trail of Cheddar Chimps on purpose. Fiona and Frieda *hadn't* ruined his brilliant plan. The girls felt a tiny bit of relief. But the relief soon vanished as they explained to Hansel and Gretel that, no, they couldn't help them. In fact, all four of them were terribly, hopelessly lost.

Chapter 4

On top of being terribly, hopelessly lost, Hansel and Gretel were starving. Fiona and Frieda were starting to get hungry, too. The four agreed that it was no use staying where they were. They set off in search of home and food.

At the same time, Fiona and Frieda wanted to be smart. After all, they knew what happened next in the fairy tale.

"Whatever you do, if you see a giant house made out of cookies, don't eat any of it," Frieda warned.

"Not even a doorknob!" Fiona added. She wagged a finger at them for emphasis.

At that, Hansel and Gretel laughed so hard they had to lean on each other to keep from falling down.

"What an excellent idea!" Gretel said at last. "A game! That will distract us from our predicament. Let's see. . . ." She put a finger on her chin and tapped her foot in an exaggerated thinking pose. "If you see a porcupine in a bunny suit, don't give it any carrots!"

"Oh, oh, I have one!" Hansel shouted. Strumming a pretend banjo, he sang, "If you see a manatee, please say hi from me."

"Stop, stop!" Fiona tried to shout over the laughter. But then, Hansel started playing a pretend kazoo, and she couldn't help laughing a little.

"Come on, we're serious," Frieda said. "A mean witch uses the candy house to trap kids, and—"

It was useless. Frieda's explanation only made Hansel and Gretel laugh even harder. Like a magic spell, their giggle fit soon spread to Fiona and Frieda. Frieda shrugged at Fiona. Fiona and Frieda knew what it meant to be helpless with laughter. There was nothing to do but let the laughter roll and crash all over them until it was all used up.

And so that was how Fiona and Frieda let down their guard in the middle of a fairy-tale emergency.

Just then, something unusual happened. A grey mouse with one white ear and big green eyes crept up to the group. If the girls hadn't felt so loosey-goosey, they would have remembered a small but important detail from the fairy tale.

In that story, a small animal leads the brother and sister to danger. But in their silly mood, Fiona and Frieda simply forgot.

"Awwwww," Fiona said, pointing at the mouse. "Look at its tiny paws."

"What a darling animal!" Gretel added. The mouse squeaked at Gretel as if in reply, which only delighted her more.

Hansel got down on his knees and, tipping an imaginary hat, said, "Howdy, Pardner."

At that, the mouse squeaked even more adorably. Then, in an almost human way, it pointed a paw toward a tunnel on the right.

"I think it wants to communicate with us," Gretel said.

The mouse seemed to nod. It pointed its tail.

It scampered toward the tunnel. Then it turned around and squeaked even more.

"Alright, alright!" Hansel laughed. "We're coming!"

And so, laughing all the way, Fiona, Frieda, Hansel, and Gretel followed the green-eyed mouse down the dark tunnel on the right. The mouse led them all the way to the end, then it turned left, and then left again, until the group saw a light up ahead.

"It's a newspaper stand!" Frieda shouted.

The others whooped in excitement and relief. A newspaper stand meant an exit must be close by. Also, newspaper stands in subways always sold snacks.

"Hello!" Fiona shouted when they got to the stand, but nobody answered. "The owner must be in the bathroom or something. I'm sure he or she will be right back."

The kids looked at the bottles of juice, soda, and chocolate milk behind the glass door of a humming refrigerator. They examined the stacks of candy bars, the bags of chips, and the jars of pickles and beef jerky. Finally, they couldn't stand it anymore.

"What if we keep track of everything we eat and pay later?" Hansel said, biting the end of a pickle. That was all the encouragement the others needed.

"You must have a salty tooth like me," Frieda said to Hansel, as she tore open a packet of potato chips.

"He does," said Gretel, "but not me. I have quite a sweet tooth, as they say." She ran her fingers along the candy bars but then stopped

Chips - 50¢
Candy - 50¢
Apple - 35¢
Water - 75¢

NO LOITERING

short. "Oooooh," she said, eyeing something behind the counter.

Then, as if being led by a string, Gretel climbed over a stack of newspapers and over the counter. "Extraordinary," she murmured.

There stood not a gingerbread house, but a gingerbread castle. It even had a moat with a fire-breathing dragon made out of green frosting and red licorice. Gumdrops, sprinkles, chocolate squares, saltwater taffy—lots and lots of candy—decorated every inch of the castle's walls and roof.

Gretel marveled at the castle for a moment. Then, without warning, she leaned over and plucked a single purple gumdrop off the pointy top of a tower. At that very moment, Fiona and Frieda finally came back to their fairy-tale senses.

"Don't eat it. It's a trap!" they both yelled.

But it was too late. As Gretel popped the gumdrop into her mouth, a horrifying sound echoed in the subway tunnel.

Aaaaaaaaah-ha-haaaa-ha-haaaaaaaaaaaa!
Aaaaaaaah-ha-ha-haaaaaaaa!

The mean witch was coming up behind
them!

Chapter 5

"**I'll get** you, my delicious doves. . . ."

The witch's high, crackly voice was getting louder and louder. The *click-click* of her running heels were getting closer and closer.

"*Aaaaaaah-ha-ha-haaaaaaaa!* I'll get you, my tender piglets, my yummy munchkins . . . and I'll eat you up!"

"Run away!" Fiona and Frieda screamed. But which way? With the witch behind them, they couldn't run back into the tunnel.

"Back here!" Gretel shouted. Just in time, she had discovered a small wooden door in the back of the stand.

"Where does it lead?" Frieda asked. She and the rest of the kids scrambled up to the open door.

"It's too dark. I can't see," Gretel said.

But it was no matter, for now the witch was inside the newspaper stand. And what a witchy witch she was—the kind of witch Frieda had been trying to imitate since her first Halloween. This witch was the real deal, though. She had a black pointy hat, black robe, long black fingernails, green skin, frizzy black hair, and a huge, hairy wart on the tip of her hideous nose.

"Enjoying some snacks, my little pudding cups?" the witch said in that mocking, sing-song way that witches always do.

"Eeeeeeeeeeeeeeeeeeek!" A loud, high wail shot out of the kids' mouths. It erupted from a screaming place so deep inside them, they didn't even know it was there.

Frieda, who was crouched down behind the rest of the group, must have shoved hard. For just then, all four of them tumbled through the small door opening.

Slam!

Just as the witch's pointy fingertips reached inside the doorway, Frieda fell against the door, closing it securely.

The closed door erased any scrap of light. The blackness seemed to crawl over their skin and creep inside their ears and up their nostrils. It rested like a weight on their chests and made them gasp. For a moment, the kids stood still, taking quick breaths of the cool, musty air.

"Fiona? Frieda? Hansel? Gretel?" They whispered each other's names and felt for hands. Once they found each other, the darkness became bearable again.

"Where are we?" Fiona and Frieda whispered to each other. In *Hansel and Gretel*, the kids never get away. Also, there's no dungeon. They were off the fairy-tale map.

"Let's find out," Fiona said. She pulled the group along a wall. Each searched for any glimmer of light—but not for long.

In the next instant, something flicked and then buzzed. A flooding brightness filled the room. The kids blinked. They looked around.

Frieda had always wondered what people meant by the expression "a cold sweat." But now she knew. As she gazed at the horrible sight, sweat beaded up all over her cold, clammy skin.

The witch smirked at them from beside the open doorway. Her hand still rested on the light switch that had made the tubes of light buzz overhead.

"I've got you now," she said, though she didn't need to waste the words. Hansel, Gretel, Fiona, and Frieda felt it like rocks in their stomachs.

Fear heightened Frieda's senses, and she noticed new details about the witch. The evil creature had a white streak in her black hair, like a skunk. Even more interesting, the witch had beautiful green eyes beneath her horrible eyebrows. To Frieda, those details seemed both out of place and familiar all at once, though she couldn't say why. She would have liked to think about it some more, but Fiona was urgently whispering something in her ear.

". . . And those are the storage lockers, see?
And the furnace . . . ,"

Frieda caught just a few words of what Fiona
was saying before the witch yelled, "Silence!"
But those few words were enough. Frieda knew
what her friend was trying to tell her. This room,
this mystery dungeon, was none other than
the basement of Castle Apartments, Fiona and
Frieda's own building.

If Frieda had the chance she would have whispered back to Fiona, "The storage lockers must be the witch's prison, and the furnace must be the stove!"

A prison and a stove are two important things in the *Hansel and Gretel* fairy tale. In that story, the witch makes Hansel her prisoner and Gretel her slave. She locks Hansel in a cage and makes Gretel bring him trays of delicious food. The witch's plan is to fatten him up and then cook him in the stove for supper.

This witch changed some details of the fairy tale, but she certainly kept the main ideas. She made Hansel and Fiona both her prisoners. With her bony fingers, she clutched their shirt sleeves and led them to an empty storage locker. She slammed the wire door so hard it shook. Then, with an evil laugh, she clicked the padlock shut.

Next, the witch turned to Frieda and Gretel. "And you, my fuzzy peaches, shall be my slaves." Her slimy lips made exaggerated Os as she relished each word. "Your job is to feed your friends until they are as plump as pumpkins. Then I shall roast them in the furnace and lick their bones clean!"

Chapter 6

The witch had set up a kitchen behind some rusty filing cabinets. Frieda and Gretel were sent there to prepare dinner. Meanwhile, Fiona sat on the floor of the storage locker hugging her knees. The girls had never been separated during a fairy-tale emergency before. They each tried to think of a plan. Without the other, though, each girl's brain felt like a bike with one broken wheel.

At last the time came for Gretel and Frieda to bring the prisoners their dinner trays.

"Frieda!" Fiona reached her hands through the wire holes of the storage locker to touch her friend's leg. Frieda put down the heaping tray. She bent down and squeezed her friend's hand.

"What are we going to do? What are we going to do?" Hansel's eyes were red from crying. Gretel reached in to stroke her brother's hair.

"Where's the witch?" Hansel asked, his voice high and wobbly.

"It's okay. She's asleep for now," Frieda answered. "We're supposed to feed you all this food through the door. We can't leave until it's all gone."

"That's good," Fiona said. "That buys us time. Besides, I'm starving." She looked at the mountain of food—frosted cookies and pretzels, doughnuts and potato chips, and other sweet and salty treats.

"How can you even think of eating?" Hansel said, hugging his stomach a little.

"Don't worry," Fiona said. She smiled at Frieda. "Everything's okay now. We're going to come up with a plan."

"Actually," Frieda said, "even in your fairy tale, you still escape—at least eventually."

"Our fairy tale?" Hansel and Gretel looked confused. Then they listened in amazement as Fiona and Frieda told them the famous story named none other than *Hansel and Gretel.*

As they spoke, the girls realized how many things about the tale didn't make sense. For example, the bone. The witch, who can't see very well, checks to see how fat Hansel is getting by ordering him to stick his finger through the prison door. But instead of using his finger, he pokes through a bone. This tricks the witch into thinking he's skinny, but how does that help him escape? Really, it just means he has to stay longer—for weeks actually—in the cage. Eventually the witch decides to eat him even if he is skinny.

"Weeks?" Hansel moaned. "I can't stand another minute!"

"Hold on!" Fiona's voice sounded impatient, but Frieda understood that her friend didn't mean to be rude. Fiona was just in the middle of coming up with a great idea and didn't want to lose it.

"The witch will only unlock this cage when she's ready to eat us, right?" Fiona said.

"Yes . . . ," Hansel slowly replied, but clearly not seeing the plan.

Both wheels of Frieda's brain were working now, too. "Which means instead of tricking the witch into thinking you're skinny we want to trick her into thinking you're fat . . . ," Frieda continued.

"But what then?" Gretel said. "Once Hansel and Fiona are out, how are we to free ourselves from her wicked grip?"

"Actually, that part's up to you," Fiona explained. Then she told how, in the fairy tale, the witch heats up the stove and tells Gretel to go up to the door and see if it's hot enough. Of course, the witch really intends to push Gretel in, but luckily Gretel is smart enough to figure out the witch's plan.

"You see," Frieda continued, "Gretel tricks the witch. She says, 'Oh, I couldn't possibly fit inside that stove. I'm far too big.' Well, the witch just has to prove her wrong. So, the witch climbs up instead. Then, in a completely told-you-so voice, the witch says, 'See? Even I can fit, and I'm far bigger than you.'"

"And those are her last words," Fiona said.

"Because then Gretel pushes her inside the stove and slams the door," Frieda added.

"You mean?" Gretel's face had gone completely white. "I . . . I . . . I . . . burn her . . . *to death?*"

Fiona and Frieda had never quite thought of it that way. But, they had to admit, that pretty much summed it up.

"I can't . . . I can't *murder* anybody." Gretel looked like she was about to throw up. Hansel didn't look so great either.

"Wait a minute!" Now Frieda sounded impatient. "There's really no reason it has to be the stove. Why not, instead of the stove, we push her—"

"Into the cage!" Fiona said.

"Exactly!" Frieda said. "After the witch lets out Hansel and Fiona, the door will be wide open."

"And she'll be standing right next to it," Fiona said.

As Fiona and Frieda worked out the details of their plan, the worry on Hansel's face slowly lifted. Eventually, he even smiled. He examined the food tray.

"Are there any Cheddar Chimps?" he asked.

"Sure thing," Frieda said.

"Pass me some, will ya?" he said. "I'm starving."

And so, the four friends feasted on the tray of treats. They finished just as the witch returned. She separated the four again and sent Frieda and Gretel to the kitchen to spend the night.

Chapter 7

His stomach full and his worries at rest, Hansel fell asleep against Fiona's shoulder. But Fiona couldn't sleep. She had an important job to do.

She dug into her pocket and pulled out her treasures from the morning—the stuffed snake, the two pens, and the sharp metal lid. She put her legs into a V and lay the items between them. Using the lid, she started sawing the snake in half. Fiona stuck out her tongue a little as she concentrated on her important task. When she was done, she held up the two pieces. They looked about the right length. She squeezed one. It would make a nice fat finger.

Of course, it needed something hard in the middle, like a bone. Next, she shoved a pen into each piece. With her eyes closed, she felt her two creations and smiled. They really did feel like nice, fat fingers with pointy fingernails.

Meanwhile, on the kitchen floor, Frieda looked down at Gretel asleep on her lap. She felt sorry for her. She felt nervous, too, because she knew how much Hansel and Gretel were counting on her and Fiona. "I won't let you down," Frieda whispered, which made her feel braver.

Frieda liked the feeling of being up late alone. Here she was in a real witch's lair, and she hadn't even had a chance to enjoy it! Keeping her legs still so as not to disturb Gretel, she leaned back against the wall and settled in to carefully observe her surroundings.

A dozen or so sputtering candles made shadows dance against the walls, while a fire raged beneath a steaming cauldron. Bottles, beakers, and jars lined the shelves and cluttered the counters. In one corner, a mass of dark green vines climbed the wall toward a small, high window. Stacks of books, each one as big as a dictionary, made strange sculptures in the dim light. Cobwebs hung in all of the right places, and dust and doom settled just so about the room.

It was a perfect witch's lair. Perhaps that is why Frieda was able to so easily spot two details that seemed strangely out of place. By Gretel's feet was a wire mesh garbage can overflowing with crinkly brown and yellow wrappers. Frieda immediately recognized them. Cheddar Chimps! Hundreds of empty bags of Cheddar Chimps. But *why?*

The other strange thing was the bowls. Tiny bowls no bigger than thimbles—in fact some of them *were* thimbles—had been carefully placed around the witch's floor. All the bowls were filled to the brim with a dark liquid.

Frieda leaned on one side to pick up a thimble. Carefully, she raised it to her nose.

Weird! Frieda would know that smell anywhere! The tiny bowls were filled with cola.

Why? That one word stuck in her mind with the insistence of a ticking clock. Cheddar Chimps and tiny bowls of soda. *Why? Why? Why?* When Frieda finally fell asleep, she dreamed that a giant question mark was chasing her.

Fiona eventually fell asleep as well. The next morning she woke up with a start at the sound of Gretel and Frieda bringing in the breakfast tray.

Fiona, Hansel, Gretel, and Frieda touched hands inside the cage. "Everybody ready?" Hansel asked.

"Yes, yes, yes, me too!" the four whispered, just as the witch entered. Then Frieda and Gretel got into position, and Fiona handed Hansel his fake finger.

"Did you enjoy your breakfast, my pretty popsicles?" the witch crooned.

"Oh boy, did we ever!" Fiona said with exaggerated gusto. She stuck out her stomach.

"I don't think I've ever been so full in my life," Hansel added. He flashed Fiona a smile.

"Excellent!" the witch said as she rubbed her fingertips together creepily. "Now then, my chunky monkeys, give Auntie Witch your finger."

"Auntie Witch?" Fiona mouthed at Frieda, who had to cover her mouth to keep from snorting.

"Come now, Auntie wants to see how fat you are," said the witch, cackling with anticipation. "Are we ready for the roaster?"

The hardest thing about the next part of the plan turned out to be trying not to laugh. First came the sight of the witch carefully squeezing the pen-and-stuffed-snake fingers like melons at the supermarket. Then came her gleeful cackling, which sounded more like a screaming pig on a roller coaster.

"Yes, yes, nice and plump. Ha-ha! Auntie has good food indeed. Indeed, indeed." The witch did a little jig. As she unlocked the cage, she continued her private chuckle. "Ha-ha! Roasted boy kabobs? Little girl chops? Kid stew? . . . Ah-ha-ha. Ah-ha-ha!"

But the next "Ah-ha-ha" didn't come from Auntie Witch. Also, it was more like an "Ah-ha-ha-who-hooooooo!" For as soon as the door was opened, Fiona and Hansel ran past the witch. Then all four kids pushed together. The witch landed smack on her bottom inside the empty storage locker.

Luckily, Fiona had a diary that locked with a padlock, so she was an expert at operating one. She snapped the lock shut well before the witch stood up and rattled the door so hard the hinges almost broke off—but didn't.

Chapter 8

Winning. It was Fiona and Frieda's favorite part of being fairy-tale superheroes.

And yet, the girls didn't even have a chance to give each other high fives or do a victory dance. For all of a sudden the witch spotted something in the corner that made her let out an evil laugh. She swooped down and picked it up. It was a Cheddar Chimp! It must have fallen on the floor during Hansel's dinner last night.

The witch popped the orange cracker into her mouth, and then without even a *poof!* she was gone. In her place was the grey mouse, the one with the white ear and green eyes.

Why hadn't Fiona and Frieda see it before? Both the witch and the mouse had the same green eyes. The witch had a white stripe in her hair; the mouse had one white ear. The mouse had led them to the witch's trap. Of course!

The mouse *was* the witch.

Inside Frieda's brain, the question marks floated away as each mystery was answered. The Cheddar Chimps! They were what made the witch turn into the mouse. And the cola! The tiny, mouse-sized bowls . . . on the floor . . . *perfect* for sipping by a scampering rodent. Cola must be what turns the mouse back into a witch!

"Grab it!" Frieda screamed. "Grab the thimble! Now!"

Frieda pointed at a thimble of cola at Hansel's feet. The mouse-witch was scurrying toward it as fast as she could.

To Frieda, the witch's plan was as clear as the answers in the back of a book. The witch had turned into a mouse to escape from the cage. Now that she was out of the cage, she meant to turn back into her usual self and—Frieda didn't even want to think about what would come after that.

Luckily, Hansel grabbed the cola just in time. But then the mouse started climbing up his legs.

"Drink it!" Frieda barked. Without so much as a raised eyebrow, Hansel followed Frieda's order.

Hansel smacked his lips. "Cola?" he asked, but this was no time for questions.

"Everyone, grab all the soda off the floor and
drink up!" Frieda screamed, pointing at the tiny
bowls.

The third graders looked like little kids at an
egg hunt as they ran frantically around the room.
But soon it became clear that all they had to do
was follow the mouse. As the mouse ran toward
a bowl, one of the four would step in front of

it, and slurp up the sweet drink. This happened
over and over again until, in the kitchen, the
mouse stopped running.

Fiona grabbed the garbage can and shook
out all the empty wrappers. Turning it over, she
slammed it over the mouse. Just to make sure,
she put a heavy book on top of the makeshift
cage.

"I think," said Fiona, catching her breath, "we just caught a very twitchy witch!"

"Way to go!" Frieda said, holding out her open hand to Fiona. *Smack!* The girls high-fived.

"A perfect ending," Fiona said. "The witch will stay a mouse forever!"

"So long as she never drinks cola," Frieda said.

"But she can have all the Cheddar Chimps she wants!" Fiona added with a giggle.

Poor Hansel and Gretel looked extremely confused. As Fiona and Frieda laughed, Hansel just scratched his head and Gretel shrugged.

Sometimes Fiona and Frieda forgot that not everyone, not even fairy-tale characters, were fairy-tale experts like them. So the girls explained everything about the witch also being the mouse and the Cheddar Chimps and the cola to Hansel and Gretel. Soon the siblings understood the full story and were laughing along with the girls.

"Come on," Fiona said, putting an arm around Gretel. "You must be so tired. Let's go upstairs and call your parents."

"Upstairs?" Hansel asked.

Frieda explained how the witch's lair was actually the basement of Castle Apartments.

"I live in 801," Fiona said.

"And I live in 802," Frieda added.

Later, as the four kids sipped hot cocoa around Fiona's kitchen table, Hansel said, "Can you believe a real mean witch was living in your basement?"

Fiona and Frieda smiled at each other. "Actually," they both said. "Yes, we can."

Then the girls explained their magic rhyming powers to the siblings. When Hansel and Gretel realized that Fiona and Frieda were fairy-tale experts, everything finally made sense.

"So that's how you knew about our fairy tale!" Hansel exclaimed.

"And it explains how you ascertained the abnormally odd circumstances under which we were captured," added Gretel.

Fiona and Frieda looked at each other and giggled. "I beg your pardon?" Fiona asked in her best manners.

All the kids laughed. "What she means is that must be how you figured out our problem—it's how you saved us!" Hansel explained.

"Yes!" both girls answered.

Hansel and Gretel's parents arrived soon after that. The grown-ups cried and cried until they had to go across the hall to Frieda's for another box of tissue. Hansel and Gretel and Fiona and Frieda promised to e-mail every day. They made plans to meet up again at Castle Apartments, since everyone already knew the way.

The next week at school, the girls brought in a great new pet for their class—a most unusual looking mouse with green eyes and one white ear. The class named their pet Mindy. (The name made the animal hide inside its toilet-paper tube until recess.)

Every day, the kids took turns feeding Mindy Cheddar Chimps and filling her water bottle. (Luckily, soda wasn't allowed in the classroom.)

And that is the story of how Fiona, Frieda, Hansel, and Gretel tricked the witch. They also found their way home and discovered a great new spot for a Halloween party—their very own basement.

The End

26. Diamond ring,
chicken wing!

7. Hula hoop...
bowl-a'-soup...

8. Fuzzy peaches,
lake leeches!

15. Halloween...
string bean...